Dear Younger Me
and Other Poems

Abigail Rocha

Dear Younger Me and Other Poems
© 2021, Abigail Rocha
All rights reserved

Edited by: April Martinez

Printed in the U.S.A
Self-Published

Cover Image: Reggie Simms
Cover Design: Virtuoso Design Studio
Website: www.virtuosodesignstudio.com

All rights reserved. No part of this publication may be reproduced, distributed, or transmitted in any form by any means, including photocopying, recording, or other electronic methods without the prior written permission of the author, except in the case of brief quotations embodied in reviews and certain other noncommercial uses permitted by copyright law.

Dedicated to mi Mama and all my brothers, thanks for teaching me about life. Also to my god-daughter, and my nieces and nephews this is for you.

Contents

Adulting Letters	......	**4**
Letters and Family	......	**32**
Letters to Teen Me	......	**44**
Letters about Love	......	**60**
Self-Empowerment Letters	......	**80**
Bilingual Poems	......	**104**
Acknowledgements	......	**159**

Adulting Letters

I submit my resignation

Titled "Adulthood declined"

Reason:

It's too difficult, more than I could have imagined.

I was thrown into this blind.

Mom and Dad! Please! I give you the ability to once again remind me, "under my roof, my rules!"

They say I have to make my **own** appointments! What a catastrophe, this can't be a normal thing.

Someone wake me from this dream. I want to go back to being a teen!

                      -Growing up is hard to do

Renuncio:

A ser adulto

Es difícil

Más de lo que creí

Mama, extraño cuando decias

"bajo mi techo mis reglas"

Esto de hacer mis propias citas

Como que no es normal

-Crecer no es lo que imagine

Dear Younger Me,

Life is not exactly what you thought it would be.

                        -I thought it would be easy

Dear Younger Me,

Did you see adults at 20 as mature and wise beings?

Not true, many are still struggling with figuring out what to do. 25 can sneak up on you and now you're in your quarter-life crisis wondering, "How can I go back and rewind time before I had a 9-5?"

-Tired Adult

Dear Younger Me,

Adulthood will be a mix of light and dark seasons. You will have everything before you, while also having nothing ahead of you. It is up to you what you do with nothing and everything life gives you.

-Looking Forward Adult

Dear Younger Me,

Being an adult will leave you wanting to be a kid again or even a teen.

-The Good Ol' Days

Dear Younger Me,

Nothing in life is perfect. You **will** make mistakes, your parents will at times disappoint. There will be things you regret. Mountains and valleys, you'll wish you never set foot. You might want to reset but it's not like in movies and shows where everything is prewritten and rehearsed. There won't always be a happy ending. Real-life does not need high ratings.

-Mistakes don't break you, they make you!

Dear Younger Me,

Adulthood is not as fun as you thought it would be. You have to do dishes, wash your clothes, and cook something different each day, or eat out of course. You will make your own money; sure, you can buy as you please! Yet don't forget you'll have more responsibilities. Mail will only be bills! Staying up late will be full of thrills, but you will need a cup of coffee in the morning to get you through the day.

–Common Sense

Dear Younger Me,

Sometimes your savings will not be enough. The income to bills ratio isn't always ideal. Be prepared to ask for help. Adults don't need to go through struggles alone.

-Seek Help it Helps

Dear Younger Me,

Live below your means, do not buy things you can't afford. Credit is **NOT** your money.

                -Just an FYI

Dear Younger Me,

Finances aren't as easy as it seems, it really takes work to figure out, plus self-control. You have to pay bills and taxes, it's all part of your adulting skills. At times you'll feel defeated but don't throw in the towel, learn to save and budget. Student loan debt: No one tells you how to navigate that. Go get scholarships!

-Paying off Debt Adult

Dear Younger Me,

Some people will be lightning fast at reaching their goals but this does not mean success. Success is being consistent and reaching your goals on your own time, not society's views on when you should have something accomplished.

-Habits form Character

Dear Younger Me,

Not everyone is going to like you. That's OK! As long as you like you. Popularity is not an adult skill. Networking, on the other hand, can help your goals be fulfilled. It's all about who you know that can help open doors for you- not about *who knows you.*

-Social Adult

Dear Younger Me,

You may have to say no to a job and quit on the spot. People are easily replaceable. Your boss will have the best interest of the company, not always for the employees. *Are you willing to compromise your peace and sanity for a paycheck?*

-Overwhelmed Adult

Dear Younger Me,

Don't wish for what you can't see. Everything may not be picture perfect. You don't know what life is like behind closed doors. People may pretend to be happy and underneath hide fears, doubts, and pain. Some may even be jealous of you, not knowing you are going through hell too.

-Grass Is Not Always as Green

Dear Younger Me,

On days you feel down and alone remember your friends the ones you can call on the phone. You can rise above whatever you are going through, don't keep it all in. You do not need to be alone in your pain, let a friend know. We all go through down moments and with each other, you can come out of it just open up to one another.

-Depressed Adult

P.S. Well... depressed in the past tense.

Dear Younger Me,

Don't be caught up in drama. Even as adults' people are fake, so be careful who you tell your life goals and dreams to. Some may betray you and, in your face, speak wonders of you. When selfish people don't know about your business they make it up for you to look bad.

-Feels like Middle School

Dear Younger Me,

No matter the age people love to gossip. It's a part of life but you can avoid it. Best response to nosy people, "it's not my business to tell."

Remember this:

**Always be loyal to those not around, it stops the gossiping from continuing and makes you a good friend to have.

-Backstabbed Adult

Dear Younger Me,

Forgive those you can. However, remember not everyone deserves your presence after.

-Keep Healthy Relationships

Dear Younger Me,

Learn to be a friend. To have friends you need to be a friend. Learn to listen without judgement. Recognize their feelings without adding your own two cents. Don't reflect the conversation to your own experience if what they need is a friend to listen. Don't assume they need advice unless they ask for it. Be 100% there, you never know they may just want to know someone cares.

–Be Understanding

P.S. You could help save a life and keep a friend.

Dear Younger Me,

You are constantly changing and your friends are also changing. There comes a time where we all are in search of our true selves. They may suddenly have new values that their 16 year old self would have not agreed with. We all grow mature and change.

-Adults Change their mind

Dear Younger Me,

You will have friends falling in love and out of love. You will have friends falling for a religion and out of a religion. Others will find the thrill of tattoos and piercings. Others will find the thrill of adventure through traveling. Some will start a career. Some will find a new career. Some will be stay at home parents. People will always be changing, don't judge. Everyone around you is attempting to figure out life. Choose to understand and when you don't or can't understand, choose to be kind.

-Being an Adult is New to Us All

Dear Younger Me,

Life can have multiple meanings depending on your perception of it. Think about when someone witnesses an event, such as a concert depending on your purchased seats. Your experience is distinct from that of someone else who was also there.

In the same way, we all may remember moments in different ways that affect each of us. Always take what best suits you in everything that you do, remember your life is not the same as your peer.

Besides, some people have privilege written on their ticket that lets their experience be completely different.

-Point of View

Dear Younger Me,

Follow through on what you say you'll do. You're parents and teachers are no longer there to hold you accountable for your actions. However, you are the one that will live with knowing you did not see something through; whether it be a small thing like keeping your car clean or big goals like quitting smoking.

-You're In Charge Now

Dear Younger Me,

Your purpose in life is not your job. You may think this because you have a job or career in which you help others or you make a difference. However, that is not your sole purpose or your sole identity. Find joy in things outside your job.

-Be You in all that you do

Dear Younger Me,

We may not all grow up to become rich and famous. Regardless, you will be successful in your own way. Look at growing up as being happy with the life you've created.

-Write Your Story

Dear Younger Me,

Adulthood means you'll finally be allowed to know the family secrets. Now you will understand the burdens your parents have kept all along. The struggles they've hidden so well. You'll finally see how much life has given and dealt them. They may have never let you feel what they felt or see what they saw until now. Give them grace they we're learning to adult too.

-Wish I did not know

Dear Younger Me,

It is not your fault, remember this! You need not carry the burdens of your parents and grandparents. Live free, don't let their mistakes affect you. Divorce, alcoholism, poverty mentality, let it go, break free of these ties. Create a new reality for your own family. You are capable of setting a new example.

-New Family Legacy

Dear Younger Me,

The uniform your parents wear is not by choice. Some parents do these jobs out of necessity but deep down in their hearts they have their own dreams and desires too. Teenage me, be present when your parents are home. Enjoy their company and the sacrifices they make for you. Those $300 for soccer or cheerleading may not have come as easily as you think. Show your parents you appreciate them. Even if you have a self-employed parent, this by far is the most difficult job.

**To you that does not have a parental figure, love and appreciate the ones you do have that show you they care.

-Appreciate the Parents in Your Life

Dear Younger Me,

Your mom's job does not define her. In her home country she would be a "licenciada en derechos" yet here in America she is more so a "licenciada en familia." She will always protect her family despite not fully speaking the language. She will continue to push forward despite being a single mom living away from familia. You will see her struggles even though she'll never admit them. You'll see how amazing and strong she is. You will reach the same adult situations she has or because of her you won't have to go through that. Show her gratitude as much as you can.

-My Superwoman

Dear Younger Me,

Don't blindly follow your elders, just because they're related to you. They may not be the best example or role model. Break away from traditions- **don't** accept things that have been passed down for generations, it may no longer apply to you.

**For *finance, business, marriage*, and other advice; seek out a mentor you see thriving in this area and pick their brains for advice. Don't seek to replicate word for word but summarize and make it your own.

-It Starts with Me

Dear Younger Me,

What do you value? Not the values of your mom, dad, grandma, brother. What do you personally value? Live by that! Make yourself proud!

-Think Independently

Dear Younger Me,

At times you will wish you can relive these moments. Death is a sure thing in life. Listen to the words of your loved ones sweetly spoken often numerously repeated. You don't want to later lament what you could have learned from them then. Not just your elders but your peers too, we are not guaranteed tomorrow. Don't get me wrong though don't ponder on sorrow. Live your life, just be wise with your time. It's more valuable than money. You'll miss the days when you could just pick up the phone and call your friend or your Grammy.

-Thinking of my Angels in Heaven

Dear Younger Me,

One of the hardest parts about being an adult is accepting the fact that your grandparents are growing older. Cherish every moment you have them on earth. Listen to every story, ask all the questions, and visit them as much as you possibly can. Don't be "too cool" to hang out with your Abuelita or your Papaw. If you can't visit them call them as much as you can. Trust me there are those who wish they had a grandma or grandpa who they can visit and learn from.

-Missing the Abuelitos

Dear Younger Me,

Si eres hispano este es para ti:

You'll hear, "Eres nacido aqui, you can be whatever you please!" Don't be offended if they disapprove of your dreams. Ellos vinieron aqui for a reason maybe for a better life for them or to provide una mejor vida para ti. It may seem that they don't support you but in reality seeing you surpass their goals will put them at ease. Keep fighting for what you want to be, despite if they disagree. The struggle is real but you can succeed and prove them it was worth it- having come to el otro lado.

-Ni de Aqui Ni de Alla

Dear Younger Me,

Your siblings may get on your nerves or be your best friend right now. Under your parents roof you'll each have your own lives and do your own things. Once you move out though, you'll be missing those times together. Prepare to call and hang out with them more now that you've got your own homes. It will definitely be much harder to work around everyone's schedules. Pray y'all have the weekends off together.

-Love You Fam

Dear Younger Me,

Holidays as an adult will be another hard part of life. Synchronizing schedules won't be easy. Unless you have a great planner in the fam. Families will become bigger, with kids, in-laws, and friends you adopt into your family. New traditions will be established. Don't reminisce on the past especially the bad times but build a new future as a family.

-Who's Cooking the Turkey?

Letters To Teen Me

Dear Younger Me,

Be careful what you sacrifice now because you cannot and will not resurrect these once they are buried. Times change, people change, you will change. What matters to you now may or may not hold its value in a few years.

                                        -Sacrificed too much

Dear Younger Me,

Enjoy these days, these will be the memories you will treasure. The friendships you build now will last or simply cause you displeasure. They can be a part of your bridal party or just a *like* on social media. It is now when these relationships will be established. Some won't even say "hi" when in the mall you pass them by. Many people will come and go. Just remember to keep those you love close.

-Reminiscing Adult

Dear Younger Me,

If I could shield you from what your eyes will see, what your ears will hear, and what your heart will feel, I would. Just know I'm proud of how much you've overcome as a teen.

-Struggle is Real but

you are stronger

Dear Younger Me,

If I could take the pain I would do that too. Unfortunately it will be different from now on. Whether it be parents' divorce, love, heartbreak, deaths, or physical pain. You will make it through. You will need all the strength you can find. Take all the time you need to heal from any of these types of heartache. There is no set timeline for your pain. If it overwhelms you though **please** don't let it consume you- let others help you through.

-Push through the pains of life

Dear Younger Me,

The choices you make now will be with you **forever** one way or another. (Emphasis on Y.O.U.) Choose your path wisely. Regardless if you make bad choices or good choices no one but **you** is allowed to bring back that part of you. Your past belongs to you and only you, never let anyone hold that over your head. Take full control of who you are and where you have come from. Build your own story and if you want to pull some pages out of that book so be it. No one is entitled to even know your mistakes, it's between you and God.

-Not letting my past define me

Dear Younger Me,

You do not need to have or live with FOMO. Every event does not need your presence, let people miss you sometimes, this way they learn to appreciate you. Not everyone you meet needs to be a part of your life; some people are meant to just pass by. Don't let others make you feel guilty. You can have time for yourself and still show your friends and family you love them.

-Have Me-Time

Dear Younger Me,

A high school diploma and/or a degree doesn't guarantee you a job. You've got to do work still to find one. Even when you find one, you may realize it does not make you happy. Don't let the fact that you went to school for that job or went through hell and back to get to this moment stop you from letting it go. You deserve to live the life you want, doing what makes you happy. Family may not be by your side and may talk down on your decisions. Let nothing hold you back from being who you've always dreamed to be! When you're 80 what story would you rather tell? How you stuck around a lousy job to make money or how you molded your life to fit your vision of success.

                                            -Think about It

Dear Younger Me,

If you are thinking about University. Listen, people will push you to go to college but won't always know how to help you get there. Look into scholarships and grants. There is a lot of free money out there, don't go into debt. Talk to your counselor. Community college is a good way to start. Classes are easier to pass and cost less, do your general ed courses there just make sure it all transfers over.

While on the college topic: Seek volunteer opportunities, make connections to build your choices for references. These will benefit you in the long run when you want to start your career.

-1st Gen Adult

Dear Younger Me,

You may graduate college later than average but you may change majors in between. That doesn't change the fact that you tried. Besides, who can be positive about what industry they would like to be in at 18?

 -Finding Yourself

Dear Younger Me,

You will also realize that college is not for everyone. Listen, some may be successful straight out of high school. They will be exactly what they are meant to be without a single degree. Perhaps even be debt-free. Your choices will make you or break you, choose wisely.

-Make Your Own Decisions

Dear Younger Me,

Your higher education will not be easy by any means, but you can do it. If you need help seek school resources, many are paid for with your tuition. Make friends in class to help you along the way. Join organizations, whether it be Greek life, business competitive clubs, or any cultural/philanthropic groups. Almost all people you meet in these orgs will graduate. Some will be in completely different fields as you. Building relationships will be great for not only your college experience but after college. Many people graduate with a degree and go into a career field outside of that discipline thanks to opportunities available through their org peers.

-Friends That Build Together

Dear Younger Me,

You have your timeline for when to succeed. You may go in a straight line with all doors opening at your feet or it may be a difficult thing. You may have to pave the way, create the road yourself, don't wait on others to do what you want to do in life. Go out there, cultivate the skills that you need and make it happen!

-Create your future

Dear Younger Me,

You can be an influencer outside of the screen. You can make a difference that doesn't need to be seen. You can make money in any way that you please. Remember your values, though, in between. You may or may not need a degree, everything you do is part of your legacy. Keep in mind there's no turning back time. You do truly reap what you sow! Plan(t) accordingly.

-I planted that seed

Dear Younger Me,

When you say "my life is ruined," think for a moment...is it? This feeling is temporary and not absolute.

                                                –Press Pause

Dear Younger Me,

Overall this is for the teenage me: Ask them to prom! Tell them you love them! Hold his hand! Give love a chance! Don't want anyone to know how you feel? You may be rejected but you can always heal. You won't get these moments back. Take that risk or learn to live with the regret of never knowing if it could have been a yes or even a kiss.

-What-If?

Letters About Love

Dear Younger Me,

Before we proceed, by now you must know life is not easy indeed. First and foremost, I ask that **you** love **yourself!** Don't be afraid of who you can be! Some may disagree, for them, in your life a spot is not guaranteed. Change comes often but loving you should be a priority. Be outspoken, take risks, advocate for what you believe. Focus on yourself!

-Riding Solo in Love

Dear Younger Me,

Did you ever imagine? Did you ever believe it? Did you ever think you'd have a baby at 15? That you'd be married at 23? It's ok, it's not always marriage and then a baby carriage. Each person has their own story, don't trouble yourself with too much worry. It may not be the perfect fairytale but it's your love story to tell.

-There are no do-overs

Dear Younger Me,

Love is not easy, it's nothing like poetry! It takes both of you to make it work. You can't be selfish and always think, "Well I'll just leave." There's more fish in the sea. You'll need to learn what it means "to love" and what it means "to be loved." Communication is not the only key; comprehension is what you need. It's a two-way street with a 0% guarantee.

       -Finding love

Dear Younger Me,

Wait don't get it twisted, at times it won't be love. Check and see for red flags. When you don't feel the butterflies in your stomach and are second-guessing yourself. Those times you will have to walk away. Abuse comes in different forms. At times disguised as cute gifts and sweet apologies. You do not deserve this! Analyze it and if you need to, run far away. It happened to me but that's only because I was being naïve. If you think you need to leave, leave. You deserve love and respect.

-Survived Abuse Adult

Dear Younger Me,

It is NOT cute, when they blow up your phone while you're out and about. Toxicity and manipulation can be hidden with empty gestures of love and constantly making you feel guilty. Retreat if they make your heart skip a beat, but out of fear.

-Pay attention to Red Flags

Dear Younger Me,

Don't romanticize the idea of someone. Love should not be like Shakespeare's Romeo and Juliet. That love story ended in tragedy. If they can't speak about you openly...think to yourself, is it love they seek or lust they can keep discreet?

-Heartbroken Adult

Dear Younger Me,

Do not glorify a toxic person.

-Manipulated Adult

Dear Younger Me,

The best advice from a wiser me...It never turns out better the second time.

-No Such Thing as a Break

Dear Younger Me,

Don't ever try to fix people. Don't date anyone with this thought or "goal" in mind. Let them fix themselves first. I'm not saying it is bad to date a broken person, we all have a past and some faults. Don't go into a relationship with this sole purpose. You won't be in love with the person, you'll be in love with who you want them to be.

-People are not projects for love

Dear Younger Me,

Don't claim no ex, leave their name and memories in the past. My mom said it best, "son ex porque los crusaste de tu corazon (they're an "x" 'cuz you crossed them out your heart), ahora son desconocidos." Trust and believe they will still stalk your socials, ask mutual friends about you. Remember who you are, especially if they broke your heart. Those days with them may have been happy ones but if it was not meant to be why keep them in your memories. Your true love deserves a clean slate and zero comparing.

-Seran Desconocidos nada de "Amigos"

Dear Younger Me,

You'll fall in love once, twice, even possibly three. Don't stress about your broken heart currently, in due time your heart will hurt less. That'll be the day you'll know what it means to be blessed. Then you can confess those three words and it will no longer scare you to death.

-Loved and Learned

Dear Younger Me,

You may see everyone around you falling in love. You may be thinking, "When will it happen to me?" I'm not here to tell you "be patient" because you'll hear that from everyone. Instead enjoy your singleness. Build your education, career, dreams, travel, or even your business. Don't envy those who have it and flaunt it. Love can be hard to find but it can also be easily lost.

-Enjoy Your Youth

Dear Younger Me,

You **will** get to see what it's like to feel love and be loved.

-Finally *In Love*

Dear Younger Me,

You will find someone who laughs thinking back on memories you've had together. Someone who will chase you back and you won't have to try and figure out if they love you. You will meet at the moment you least expect it. It will come so natural that you will feel you've known them your whole life. Those adults who say "When I found the one, I just knew." It may sound fake something only for fairytales but it's true. When your love comes you will know too!

                                -Give Love to be loved

Dear Younger me,

Learn to read your partners love languages. Each person is different and deserves to be shown love in the way they most need and appreciate it.

-Love them

Dear Younger Me,

You will hear many people say they married their best friend. This may happen at their courting stage when they are still getting to know each other. Some will become best friends once they are already married that's love for you, it's never the same love story. We all are unique and you will find your person.

-You Will be Best Friends

Dear Younger Me,

Love is worth it. Also, choose your side of the bed wisely it is yours forever.

-Dreaming Together

Dear Younger Me,

You may have nothing at first. You may both have a 9-5 or grave yard shifts just to make it by. Be patient, adulting is hard especially being married and adulting. Trust each other. Build together. Love each other. One day you'll look back and see how far you've come together. It is most definitely hard but quitting is not an option when you both give it your all in love.

-Starting from Zero

Dear Younger Me,

Marriage is beautiful but it is not easy. In movies you always see the <u>big wedding</u> you never see the effort and hard work it takes <u>to be married</u>. Love will carry you so far. You will need to make choices together, tough ones and easy ones. Even with or without kids they will be your family. Take care of what you build together.

    -You,

        That is all I

        desire

        Always

Self-Empowerment Letters

Dear Younger Me,

There are many things you cannot control. Life is a literal rollercoaster. You'll have to learn to set your pride aside and accept your failures. Don't live a life of regrets, accept that at times you will be upset. Failing is not as bad as they make it seem, failing can even lead you to reach your dreams. You'll need to acknowledge which decisions will lead you closer to your goals and which ones wont, let those go. You may have to build your steps as you climb the lopsided staircase of life.

-Live and Learn

Dear Younger Me,

Be teachable. How can you grow if you don't accept feedback or listen to others who know and have been there already? Be mindful of who you accept advice from. Some people give advice with themselves in mind. Careful accepting things that benefit others more than you.

-Learn and Grow

Dear Younger Me,

This may be a hard pill to swallow but sometimes you'll have to pause and ask- "Am I the Problem?" If it is you, accept your faults, then reflect and redirect your thoughts and attitude. Constructive criticism can help you improve if you choose to accept it. Most adults have difficulty accepting responsibility for their actions. Don't be one of those. Ask yourself- "How can I do better?"

-Maybe YTA

Dear Younger Me,

Some things will be out of your control. When you're stuck in this moment try not to react instead recognize what you are capable of and act accordingly. Despite your best efforts, there will be times where you'll just have to move on and take comfort knowing you did all that you could.

 -I cannot control the weather

Dear Younger Me,

There will be situations you will try to forget but your mind won't let go. Pause, reflect, keep moving forward don't stay and soak in those thoughts. You may cringe at things you've done but the sun does not stop at sunrise it sets at some point in the day and rises again the next. Life is painfully hard yet beautiful too, each new morning gives you a chance to reset.

-Try Again

Dear Younger Me,

In moments of anxiety, panic, fear. Don't do it alone it is not an easy road. We all go through those speed bumps even if most won't admit it. You deserve someone to help you get through, I know I really did.

-You've Got a Friend in me

Dear Younger Me,

Time is more precious than money. People are gone in a flash. One day you'll wish you had more time but will no longer be able to press play or rewind.

-What matters to me?

Dear Younger Me,

Un-forgiveness will keep you in the past. Let it go and don't let the past live in your thoughts. Be present, enjoy the current happy moments of life. You cannot change the past anymore. Focus on your next move instead and live for today not yesterday's lost battles.

-Grudges Keep Memories Alive

Dear Younger Me,

Be cautious, always be aware of your boundaries. It's your life. You choose what moments to share and with who. People will seek to find out how far they can go before you put a stop to them. No one is entitled to you and your time or kindness.

-Have Been Nice for Too Long

Dear Younger Me,

There are three parts to the truth:

1) Their side of the story
2) Your side of the story
3) The real story

Be careful what and who you believe.

Think about the information... is it something that will ultimately benefit you? If no, then take it with a grain of salt. There will be things you will never fully know the whole truth to. You'll need to live with what side you choose. Families and friendships can end by choosing not to believe or comprehend what is said.

-The Hurt Adult

Dear Younger Me,

There are three types of fears:

1) Fear of uncertainty

2) Fear of being uncomfortable

3) Fear of a noun

How do you overcome these fears?

1) Experiences build you up.

2) Take risks, you'll never know what you're capable of unless you try.

3) Don't let this hold you back from living the life you desire. Take action.

-Live Fearless

Dear Younger Me,

Don't lose to fear, overcome it. Even with fear whispering in your ear, do it anyway!

-What's stopping you?

Dear Younger Me,

Even if your voice shakes.

Even if you cry when you are angry.

Speak up!

It takes courage but it's better than being screwed over.

-Advocate for Yourself

Dear Younger Me,

Sometimes to make a difference in this world you have to start with you. If you will change, everything will change around you and for you.

**Remember...whatever you focus on you elevate!

-Elevate Your Dreams

Dear Younger Me,

"Someday" and "One day" are not days of the week. Visualize tomorrow, use that as your motivation to get things done today.

-Procrastinating is not a good Habit

Dear Younger Me,

You'll be in need sometimes. Let your body and mind get what it needs. Place your pride aside and accept the help. Rest days are needed.

-I Need to Eat

#Spiritually

#Mentally

#Physically

Dear Younger Me,

You will be the one that has to live with the consequences of what you put into your body <u>and</u> what you do with your body. Practice self-care with your skin, teeth, hair, body, and mind.

-Mindful Adult

Dear Younger Me,

I do apologize for all the pain I put you through. Was it worth it, yes? After all it made me who I am today. Sorry for the times I cried myself to sleep wondering if someone would ever love me. Dear body sorry for the carelessness- I promise I'll accept you today. Took me a long time to really be me. I'm proud of how far we've come. I'll keep working on me daily.

-Embraced Reality

Dear Younger Me,

When you were 5, do you remember how wild your dreams could be? Astronaut, doctor, lawyer, mom, chef, an artist, even possibly a trapeze.

Keep that magic alive and don't let adulting give your dreams even a slight chance to die. Simple projects and hobbies can become your ideal job, business, or income. If you've got the drive to keep moving forward despite the awkward and scary times, follow through and make it happen. No one else is responsible for your passion but you.

-Dream, as if you're 5

Dear Younger Me,

Have you heard of the man inside the belly of a fish? This man was running away from his fears and from his calling. Don't be that man or woman. Stand up to your doubts and fears! If you feel the need to run away, run but towards what scares you. You never know what good may come out of it.

-Born for Such a Time as This

Dear Younger Me,

Write something. Be an author. They may judge you but who are they to hold you back. The first book is just to get your foot in the door. Writing is not meant to go viral; it's meant to be impactful. A rough draft or bestseller you need a place to begin.

-Aspiring Writer

Dear Younger Me,

Last but not least, life does not come with a guarantee. You just have to take a chance to see what you can be. No matter what, it always gets better as each day goes by, I promise.

                    -Take a Leap of Faith

Bilingual Poems

Pensamientos

Todo lo que me proponi, lo cumpli

Y no es para presumir, sino que es como mi vida viví y aún sigo así...

Sin miedo

Aunque aveces falle

Y mi nombre e imagen la gente quisieron destrozar

Aun asi me levante, aprendí de mis batallas

Y crecí un poco mas cada dia

Y sigo aqui

Pa' delante

Dear Younger Me

This goes to the songs I never wrote

The lyrics stuck in a post-it note

Notepads filled with tears and maybe only three words.

This goes to the risks I never took

The mistakes I foresaw and chose to simply withdraw.

Memories I wish

Could now fade away

Yet have made me who I am today.

This goes to the poems I chose not to share

The notebooks filled with scribbles and endless

Quotes silenced there

This goes to the real me.

The one I've been hiding, down deep.

Let your voice be free!

Who knows maybe you can inspire another ME.

(1)

El aire

Cuenta tus tristezas

Susurra tu pasado

En esta noche tenebrosa

Tus heridas en las nubes vuelan

El viento cesará

Y la luz de la luna

Brillara

tus

lagrimas pronto

desapareceran

y podras

el dolor

olvidar

y de la vida

gozar

(1)

This dreary night

Whispers the chilling

miseries of your past

The clouds

Make known

your pain

in their gloomy

dance tonight

The wind will soon cease

And the light of the moon

Will shine through

Dry your tears

as the clouds fade away

once again you'll shine

like the starlit

purple night sky

(2)

Porque escribirle al amor

Cuando la vida tiene una gran voz

Que habla de logros y caídas

Distintos viajes te dan las experiencias

En esta vida

Rectificando o enderezando lo que significa ser

(2)

Why must we write about love?

When life has such a loud voice

Speaks of success and failure

Each leading you down a different path

(3)

Quisiera poder sentir las olas
Que creas al bailar
Y así poder admirar

Quisiera poder tocar las estrellas
Que dejaste al seguir tus suenos
Mientras a mi me olvidaste

(3)

If only I could smell the roses
The ones you planted with desire
If only I could feel the waves
As you danced and I admired

If only I could touch those stars
The ones you left behind as you
Left me aside to reach your goals

(4)

Empiezo de nuevo

a escribir otro cuento

un poco nublado

mis pensamientos

an estado

(4)

My thoughts have been cloudy lately

But

Now

I begin a new story

As the clouds drift slightly

I see a silver lining

(5)

Me he perdido a mi mismo

No se quien es el verdadero yo

Quiero saber lo que se siente ser feliz

Siempre he sido definido

Por el pasado que cargo conmigo

(5)

I've lost myself

I haven't a clue of the real you

Wait I mean, the real me

I'd like to know

I'd like to see

I no longer want to be

Defined

By the burdens I've carried

I just want to be free

To be me

(6)

Ayi en desesperación

Te encontre ansiedad

Ayi en silencio

Te encontre humildad

Ayi en tu amor

Encontré la felicidad

En distintas fases encontré

El significado

De lo que nunca he buscado

Y a lo que no le he pedido solicitud

(6)

In despair

I found anxiety

In the silence

I found humility

In your love

I have found happiness

In these phases of life I found

A significant amount

Of feelings I never searched for

Moments I never requested

Yet have arrived

(7)

Si fuera ancla

En la tempestad

De la vida

No te soltaria

Te daria lo que necesitarás

Para ver tu alegria

y no dejaria que

nadie te lastimara

la luna seria mi testigo

de como seria yo tu protección y abrigo

las olas vendran

pero tu a salvo estarás

siempre la niña de mis ojos

mi bebe hermoso

(7)

If I were an anchor

In the storm

Of life

I would not lift my hold

Seeing you smile and be bold

I'd keep you stable

I would never

Let anyone hurt you

The moon as my witness

I'd provide you with shelter

The waves may come

Safe, you'd be in my protection, my arms

My baby

Forever the apple of my eye

(8)

Llegaste a mi vida

Como el sol por la mañana

que tan fuerte brilla

Te dije mejor otro día

Pero Tu Luz resplandecía

Y no pude dejarte ir

(8)

You came into my life one day
Shinning like the morning sun
I whispered for you to go away
I said not today
But you shined your light brighter
and I could not help but let you stay

(9)

Insistías al buscarme

Pero me mentiste

Decías que me amabas

Pero con mi mente y emociones jugabas

Me culpabas de tus enojos

Celos, gritos, y humillación

Ya no mas latía por ti mi corazón

El amor se destrozó

Y de ti al fin huí

Ahora feliz

Soy

Sin ti

(9)

How did you become so distant?

The love we shared became
inconsistent

Irrelevant, fake, too much persistence

You held my hand so sweet

but in my head it spelled out defeat

and my heart lost the love it beat

For you and I in my mind

walked from earth to heavens skies

but your jealousy overcame you

the love I had disappeared

as you stated I was the one to blame

for all the anger you held

thankfully I got away

I'm much happier today

(10)

Mil pensamientos tengo

Te perdimos

Tu alma voló por el viento

Solo recuerdos quedan

De tus sonrisas y alegrías

Odio saber que no te vi por mucho tiempo

Te busco en las miradas de otros

Tu sonrisa nunca olvidaré

Tu memoria en mi corazón siempre llevaré

(10)

I think of you daily

Memories words and tons of maybes

I hate that you're gone

I hate knowing I had not seen you in so long

I see you in everyone your age

that silly smile on your face

your memory forever in our hearts

never forgotten unfortunately apart.

(11)

Las personas no entienden

No comprenden

Lo que es ser una rosa en

Campo de girasoles

Se burlan de tus pétalos

Te humillan

Será ignorancia o no comprenderán

Lo que es ser rosa

En esta sociedad

De girasoles

No saben que las espinas son tu proteccion

Girasoles llegaron mas alto mas rapido

Pero con mis petalos y espinas

Tambien puedo lograrlo

Conozco mis raíces

Aunque sean de otros países

Soy una rosa y soy fuerte

(11)

I see their expressions daily
They don't or just won't
Understand
What it feels to be a rose in
A field of sunflowers

Standing alone

They make jokes of my petals
my stem they try to break
trying to intimidate
They forget about my thorns
My protection

In a society of sunflowers
I know my roots
I'm a rose and I am strong
I too can reach the sky

(12)

Ser jefe

Ser dueño

Ser alguien es lo que me dan a comprender

Pero nunca me contaron lo difícil que es

Mucha gente, tu propia sangre

Te tiran piedras y no dejan que

Tus sueños arranquen

"Eres nacido aquí"

Uy esa frase

Es difícil aunque soy de aquí

Porque muchos no creen en mi

Y no ay muchos a los que puedo seguir

Dia a dia, mi propio camino tengo que construir

¿Sera mas facil para mis hijos

En los años por venir?

(12)

Be the boss

Reach your dreams

Be somebody

I hear these words from everybody

No one told me this,

is the most difficult road.

Yet I chose to take it

Tons of people "rooting" for you

But also whispering behind your back

Hoping you won't get there

"You have tons of opportunities

You were born here!"

It's true but look at the few.

There aren't many I can seek

To help me at each peak

I had to build my own steps as I climbed

I wonder if it will be easier for my children

In the years to come

(13)

En la sombra del ayer

Encuentras las metas de hoy

Las piedras que tropece

Ahora puedo a otros

Prevenir

No es algo facil

Yo lo logre

Tu puedes tambien

Solo recuerda donde yo tropece

Tu dale la vuelta y no caigas

tambien

(13)

in the shadows of yesterday

loom the visions of today

the steps I tripped over

now visible obstacles,

I can warn others

It's not an easy climb

I made it

So can you

Just learn from my mistakes.

That'll help you

Get through

(14)

Yo intentando y no puedo

Describir:

Lo que siento.

Tampoco hacia donde me dirijo.

Pido a la luna

¿se mi brujula?

Guia mis pasos

Hacia donde

Puedo encontrar la felicidad

(14)

I try

But

I can't describe

How I feel

Can't even describe

Where I'm headed

Light of the moon

I ask you tonight

Be my guide

My compass

Direct my steps

To where

Happiness

Is

(15)

De niño

Ya veía este tiempo venir

Con ancias queria poder estar aqui

...

Porque a los dieciocho

Tengo estas decisiones

Tan grandes y tan pequeñas

...

¿Porque ser adulto

Es tan difícil?

Dios devuelveme el tiempo

prefiero ser niño denuevo

(15)

Every child dreams

Of the day they are no longer a kid or teen, but

At 18 who would have dreamt

An adult I'd be

Decisions

From small to great

I'd have to make

This is more difficult

Than I could have believed

Take it back please

I'd rather be

A kid again

(16)

Estoy alucinando

Sera que eres tu

O un espejismo en el desierto

Bailando

De aqui pa'ya y de alla pa'ca

Y luego tu bello canto

No se si podre resistir

Como en la Odisea,,

¿Sera,

que me quieres encantar?

(16)

is it you?

am I hallucinating?

is this real?

or a mirage in the desert?

your body sways

like a flower bending in the breeze

I hear violins

or is it sirens?

Enchanting me

Like in the Odyssey

(17)

Si podria

Empezar de Nuevo

Regresar al momento zero

Donde tu y yo

Desconocidos somos

Evitaria enamorarme

De ti

Y mi Corazon

No tendria que sufrir

(17)

If I could start a new

Back to the day

We were mere strangers

Back before our hearts

Became one

And

I could spare the pain

Of meeting the one that got away

(18)

La tierra tiembla

El aire ruge

El amor por ti

Se disuelve

Como la naturaleza

Actua sin explicacion

Tambien asi el Corazon

(18)

The earth trembles

The wind rages

My love for you

Deteriorates slowly

Just like nature

Happens

Without an explanation

My heart

Makes decisions

Without my minds consideration

(19)

Trate de esquivarte
Pero como amigos quedamos
Pensando mas y mas en ti
Y al fin te dije que si
Me enamoraste

...

Envejecer a tu lado
Es todo lo que ahora deseo

(19)

I tried to avoid you

The feelings,

I tried to hide.

We became friends

My mind could not

Stop thinking of you

At last I gave in

For you I fell

And now all I can think of

Is growing old

With you

By my side

That is all I desire

(20)

Lo que siento contigo

Es algo que aun no creo

Y con pocas palabras puedo describir

Te imagine asi desde antes de conocerte

Y hasta viejitos con muchos hijos

Quiero contigo la vida vivir...

(20)

"I love you"

Is not enough to describe

What I feel

I want to grow old together

Have our children and grandchildren

See what you can build with love

Even though we are only 21

(21)

De vez en cuando

Aparece denuevo este vacio

En mi Corazon

Y mi mente

Reflejando mi pasado

Queriendo borrar mi felicidad

Intentando mentirme a mi misma

Busco vicios vacios

Ahogando mis sentimientos

Y aun asi sigo con mi carita feliz

Preguntame

Te contestare

"Todo esta bien"

Y a la vez quisiera gritar

Y reclamarle al mundo entero

Ni yo misma se lo que quiero

(21)

At times my mind and corazon

Both lie to me

I find myself in a flowing stream

Of deafening thoughts

Trying to pull me back

Trying to bury me deep

In this pit of self-loathing

Lies that- I'm not worth loving

Lies that-I'm not truly living

Ask me

I'll simply reply

"I'm ok"

(22)

Esperaba con dolor

Y ancias

Este dia

El dia en que al fin

Pudiera pensar en ti

Y sentir nada

Ni una lagrima derramar

Y al fin mi Corazon ya no mas

Podrias lastimar

(22)

I couldn't wait for the day

I could think of you

And feel no pain

(23)

En ese momento encontre paz

No mas era una niña de dieciseis

Con miedo al futuro

Y buscando ser amada y adorada

Solo tarde unos años para realizarlo

Bueno, para averiguarlo

Que en esos dulces dieciseis años

Ya era libre, para crear mi futuro

Y crear mi propia historia

Sin juzgarme a mi misma

Sin renegarle al pasado

Sin tantas heridas

Sin pensar en promesas quebrantadas

O como volver y poder recoger

La Mirada de ella

Y dejarla saber

Lo que habria por venir

Lo que algun dia la haria tan feliz

(23)

In that moment I found peace

A trip I was too nervous to take

Made me realize

I was no longer that little girl

Sixteen

Wanting so bad to be loved

Not realizing how in those teen years

I was already free

It only took me a few years to see

What it meant to be me

If I could go back and give her this message

Let her know how her life would shine

It would not be what she expected

But

Would make her

Understand what happiness is

(24)

En estos dias

Nublados

recuerdo

Los momentos

De adolescentes

Cuando una sola llamada

Nos llevaba a unas aventuras

En esta ciudad

Nos sentiamos invencibles

En nuestros carros convertibles

Viajando a nuestro propio ritmo

Quien nos viera hoy

Ojala nunca olvidemos

Los sueños y pasion de esos años

Sigamos echandole ganas plebes

Seguro algun dia triunfaremos

Y todo valdra la pena

(24)

I remember our teenage years
Riding in speeding cars
Thinking we were invincible
In our convertibles
How did we survive?
Those wild rollercoaster rides
Thank God I didn't die
Before I got to show
The world
My purpose
My fight
My reasons to live
My Why

(25)

Rodeate de gente que te ama

No sabras cuando Dios te llame a casa

Vive tu vida

Tal vez algun dia

Podran contar tus

Chistes e historias

Y te recordaran con alegria

(25)

Surround yourself with those that love you

You don't know when God will say you're due

Live your life

You won't get to do it twice

(26)

Para mis abuelas en el cielo

Las amo y las quiero

Tanto me enseñaron

Su legado nunca sera olvidado

Gracias por siempre mis llamadas contestar

Y por todas las historias y consejos

Que nos solian dar

Porque siempre en sus casitas

Podiamos llegar sin avisar

Y con un abrazo contar.

(26)

I inherited your wavy hair

Your accent I wish I had inherited that too

You left your family, your country

Your ranch and all your cattle

To live in LA

Through the struggles

The language gap

Somehow you raised kids and grandkids

Who grew up not only bilingual but bicultural

You said we all made you proud

But YOU

Is who

I am proud of

You were braver than I am

Leaving it all behind

To never return

Making this new land your home

Acknowledgements

Special Thanks:
> To my husband who listened to my never ending inspirational music while I wrote these pages. Who also reviewed my poems and letters even when I only changed a single word. Thanks for always making me smile and for always supporting my dreams.
> To my editor and best friend! I don't think I would have been able to see this through without you! Thank you for pushing me to see this through.
> To the designer of the cover, fellow poet, and friend thank you for making this project's words come to life through your art.
> To my Friends/Instagram followers for answering my questions and inspiring some of the letters and poems: Vixies, Yanet, Alba, Priyanka, Consuelo, Adriana, Marysol, JR, My Bigg
> **To my familia los amo!!!**

Made in the USA
Monee, IL
11 November 2021